Illustrations copyright © 2017 by Pamela Dalton.
All rights reserved. No part of this book may be reproduced in any form
without written permission from the publisher.

Library of Congress Cataloging-in-Publication Data:
Dalton, Pamela (Illustrator), illustrator, compiler.
Under the silver moon : lullabies, night songs & poems
illustrated by Pamela Dalton.
pages cm
Summary: Cut-paper artist Pamela Dalton presents a collection of classic
lullabies, traditional children's songs, and poetry.
ISBN 978-1-4521-1673-0
1.Children's songs. 2.Lullabies. 3.Nursery rhymes. 4.Bedtime—Songs and music.
5.Bedtime—Juvenile poetry. [1.Songs. 2.Lullabies. 3.Nursery rhymes. 4.Bedtime—
Songs and music. 5.Bedtime—Poetry.] I.Title.

PZ8.3.D1773Un 2015
782.42—dc23
[E]
2014036137

Manufactured in China.

MIX
Paper from
responsible sources
FSC™ C104723
FSC
www.fsc.org

Design by Amelia Mack and Molly Fehr.
Typeset in Hightower and Aphrodite.
The illustrations in this book were rendered in cut paper and watercolor.

10 9 8 7 6 5 4 3 2 1

Handprint Books
An imprint of Chronicle Books LLC
680 Second Street
San Francisco, California 94107
www.chroniclekids.com

Under the Silver Moon

Lullabies, Night Songs & Poems

ILLUSTRATIONS BY

Pamela Dalton

HANDPRINT BOOKS

AN IMPRINT OF CHRONICLE BOOKS • SAN FRANCISCO

Oh, how lovely is the evening, is the evening,
When the bells are sweetly ringing, sweetly ringing!
Ding, dong, ding, dong, ding, dong.

—TRADITIONAL GERMAN ROUND

I See the Moon

I see the moon, the moon sees me
Shining through the leaves of the old oak tree
Oh, let the light that shines on me
Shine on the one I love.

Over the mountain, over the sea,
Back where my heart is longing to be
Oh, let the light that shines on me
Shine on the one I love.

I hear the lark, the lark hears me
Singing from the leaves of the old oak tree
Oh, let the lark that sings to me
Sing to the one I love.

Over the mountains, over the sea
Back where my heart is longing to be
Oh, let the lark that sings to me
Sing to the one I love.

—TRADITIONAL NURSERY RHYME

Twinkle, twinkle, Little Star

Twinkle, twinkle, little star,
How I wonder what you are.
Up above the world so high,
Like a diamond in the sky.
Twinkle, twinkle, little star,
How I wonder what you are.

—JANE TAYLOR, 1806

All the Pretty Little Ponies

Hush a bye
Don't you cry
Go to sleep my little baby
When you wake
You shall have
All the pretty little ponies

In your bed
Momma said
Baby's riding off to dreamland
One by one
They've begun
Dance and prance for little baby
Blacks and bays, dapples and grays
Running in the night

When you wake
You shall have
All the pretty little ponies

—TRADITIONAL AMERICAN,
POSSIBLY AFRICAN AMERICAN, LULLABY

My Bed Is a Boat

My bed is like a little boat;
Nurse helps me in when I embark;
She girds me in my sailor's coat
And starts me in the dark.

At night I go on board and say
Good-night to all my friends on shore;
I shut my eyes and sail away
And see and hear no more.

And sometimes things to bed I take,
As prudent sailors have to do;
Perhaps a slice of wedding-cake,
Perhaps a toy or two.

All night across the dark we steer;
But when the day returns at last,
Safe in my room beside the pier,
I find my vessel fast.

—ROBERT LOUIS STEVENSON

The White Seal's Lullaby

Oh! hush thee, my baby, the night is behind us,
And black are the waters that sparkled so green.
The moon, o'er the combers, looks downward to find us
At rest in the hollows that rustle between.

Where billow meets billow, there soft be thy pillow;
Ah, weary wee flipperling, curl at thy ease!
The storm shall not wake thee, nor shark overtake thee,
Asleep in the arms of the slow-swinging seas.

—RUDYARD KIPLING

Baby Sleeps at Home

Hush! the waves are rolling in,
White with foam, white with foam;
Father toils amid the din;
But baby sleeps at home.

Hush! the winds roar hoarse and deep,
On they come, on they come!
Brother seeks the wandering sheep;
But baby sleeps at home.

Hush! the rain sweeps o'er the knowes,
Where they roam, where they roam;
Sister goes to seek the cows;
But baby sleeps at home.

—GAELIC LULLABY

Funny Ways

Some things go to sleep in such a funny way:
Little birds stand on one leg and tuck their heads away;

Chickens do the same standing on their perch;
Little mice lie soft and still as if they were in church;

Kittens curl up close in such a funny ball;
Horses hang their heads and stand still in a stall;

Sometimes dogs stretch out or curl up in a heap;
Cows lie down upon their sides when they would go to sleep.

But little babies dear are snugly tucked in beds,
Warm with blankets all so soft, and pillows for their heads.

Birds and beast and babe—I wonder which of all
Dream the dearest dreams that down from dreamland fall!

—UNKNOWN (EARLY 20TH CENTURY AMERICAN)

Matthew, Mark, Luke, and John

Matthew, Mark, Luke, and John,
Bless this bed that I lie on.
Four corners to my bed;
Five angels there be spread:
Two at my head, two at my feet,
One at my heart, my soul to keep.

—TRADITIONAL PRAYER

Brahms' Lullaby

Lullaby and good night, with roses bedight,
With lilies o'er spread is baby's wee bed.
Lay thee down now and rest, may thy slumber be blessed.
Lay thee down now and rest, may thy slumber be blessed.
Lullaby and good night, thy mother's delight;
Bright angels beside my darling abide.
They will guard thee at rest, thou shalt wake on my breast.
They will guard thee at rest, thou shalt wake on my breast.

—TRADITIONAL GERMAN LULLABY

Hush, Little Baby

Hush, little baby, don't say a word,
Papa's gonna buy you a mockingbird.

And if that mockingbird won't sing,
Mama's gonna buy you a diamond ring.

And if that diamond ring turns brass,
Papa's gonna buy you a looking glass.

And if that looking glass gets broke,
Mama's gonna buy you a billy goat.

And if that billy goat won't pull,
Papa's gonna buy you a cart and bull.

And if that cart and bull turn over,
Mama's gonna buy you a dog named Rover.

And if that dog named Rover won't bark,
Papa's gonna buy you a horse and cart.

And if that horse and cart fall down,
You'll still be the sweetest little baby in town.

—TRADITIONAL AMERICAN NURSERY RHYME

Dance, Little Baby

Dance, little baby, dance up high;
Never mind, baby, mother is by;
Crow and caper, caper and crow,
There, little baby, there you go;
Up to the ceiling, down to the ground,
Backwards and forwards, round and round;
Dance, little baby, and mother shall sing,
With the merry gay coral, ding-a-ding, ding.

—TRADITIONAL NURSERY RHYME

Sweet and Low

Sleep and rest, sleep and rest,
Father will come to thee soon;
Rest, rest, on mother's breast,
Father will come to thee soon;
Father will come to his babe in the nest,
Silver sails all out of the west
Under the silver moon:
Sleep, my little one, sleep, my pretty one, sleep.

—ALFRED, LORD TENNYSON

Sleep, Baby, Sleep

Sleep, baby, sleep,
Thy father guards the sheep,
Thy mother shakes the little trees,
There falls down one little dream.
Sleep, baby, sleep!

Sleep, baby, sleep,
The sky draws the sheep,
The little stars are the little lambs,
The moon, that is the little shepherd,
Sleep, baby, sleep!

Sleep, baby, sleep,
I shall give you a sheep
With one fine golden bell,
That shall be thy journeyman,
Sleep, baby, sleep!

—TRADITIONAL GERMAN RHYME

Evening Prayer

When at night I go to sleep
Fourteen angels watch do keep
Two my head are guarding,
Two my feet are guiding,
Two are on my right hand,
Two are on my left hand,
Two who warmly cover,
Two who o'er me hover,
Two to whom 'tis given
To guide my steps
To heaven

Sleeping sofly, then it seems
Heaven enters in my dreams;
Angels hover round me,
Whisp'ring they have found me;
Two are sweetly singing,
Two are garlands bringing,
Strewing me with roses
As my soul reposes.
God will not forsake me
When dawn at last will wake me.

—ENGELBERT HUMPERDINCK

"Let's go to bed,"
Says Sleepy-head;
"Let's stay awhile," says Slow;
"Put on the pot,"
Says Greedy-sot,
"We'll sup before we go."

—TRADITIONAL NURSERY RHYME

Diddle, diddle, dumpling, my son John,
Went to bed with his trousers on;
One shoe off, and the other shoe on,
Diddle, diddle, dumpling, my son John.

—TRADITIONAL NURSERY RHYME

Sweetly Sleep

Hush my baby, sweetly sleep
Do not cry
I will sing a lullaby
I will rock you, rock you, rock you
I will rock you, rock you, rock you
Feel my arms that keep you warm
Snuggling around your tiny form
Precious baby, sweetly sleep
Sleep in peace

Sleep in comfort, slumber deep
I will rock you, rock you, rock you
I will rock you, rock you, rock you
Close your eyes my darling one
'Til the new day has begun
I will rock you, rock you, rock you
I will rock you, rock you, rock you
Sleep in peace 'til day has come
Darling, darling, little one

—TRADITIONAL CZECH CAROL,
TRANSLATED BY PERCY DEARMER

Peace

Peace I ask of thee o river,
Peace, peace, peace.
E're I learn to live serenely,
Cares will cease.
From the hills I gather courage,
Visions of the day to be.
Strength to lead and strength to follow,
All are given unto me.
Peace I ask of thee o river,
Peace, peace, peace.

—TRADITIONAL SONG

This one's for the boys—
Elijah Bleu and Sebastian Francis

—PAMELA DALTON